Our lov. ͜ ͜ ͜

Art by

www.artfromthecrypt.co.uk

Double or Quits

Prequel to

The Chronicles of Halvar & Clarence

Written By J.D. Gammie

PRIME OF PAN-TERRA

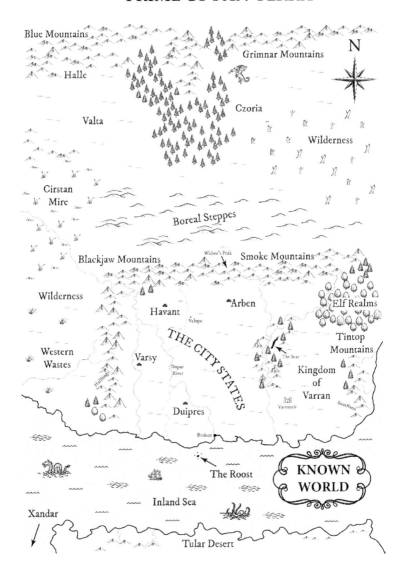

Chapter 1

In the inky-black subterranean passage, guttering light spat from the oak stump that was the last remnant of the torches they had brought into the mountain. Shadows danced across the dun-hued rock walls of the accursed tunnel as Veritas tried to think. The priest blamed himself, again and again. Smoky flame obscured his sight, but it was not the reason for the tears that started in his eyes. Legs finally giving way, slumping to the ground, he wept. Broken and cold, he had utterly failed his liege.

The man whose father had clothed him, took him in and assisted his rise in the holy order. The man whom he had chased around the transept as a boy, little legs pumping as he giggled and fled. Veritas shuddered as reverberating and cascading through his fractured mind he heard the inhuman scream that had issued from the Lord Marshall's mouth… as, as… the abominable spectral hand had emerged from Alfric's chest! Veritas felt his mind slipping back into terror. The leering, gloating in the hell spawn's pallid face… a Lord of Corpses, the adversary! Here?! How could that be? This was an expedition to clear the hills of vermin; dogmen and trolls…

Why had his god abandoned him? That bitterness, the desertion and loss, cast him adrift in a sea of midnight much darker than these earthly caverns.

'Nnnooo…' the priest moaned as he sank once more to the hard-packed earth. He had fled into the stygian black of the nearest tunnel, feet pounding, chest heaving. Too terrified to scream, nothing but the dread and horror lending strength to his failing limbs. How many others had escaped? To his eternal shame, he had thought of nothing and no one in his desperate flight. Now, he was he knew not where. There were several exits to the crypt that they had uncovered. This was not that which they had entered by, but Veritas *would not* go back.

In truth, he was not sure of the way. In haste he had passed through ancient archways, stumbled down lichen-matted steps and plunged through other half-seen forbidding portals, reflexively choosing anything that seemed farthest from the terror behind. Heart thumping in his breast, Veritas tried to listen now.

Did anyone else get out? Will they come this way?

Silence.

His staccato breaths were the only sound. Utterly lost, the oppressive weight of the cold stone above him robbed him of all hope. Most hideously, the tenebrous darkness leached away his inner light, his connection to The Lady… his salvation. Thoughts beginning to unravel, Veritas sat alone with his dread.

***

Lord Alfric's men shouted their consternation:

'Bodies, my Lord!'

Hastily they backed towards the entrance to the large, dome-ceilinged room they had just entered. Veritas craned his neck to see past them and could make out an enormous black basalt altar, carved with strange runes which made his eyes recoil. Lit only by the smoky flame of their torches, they seemed to writhe with life. It felt as if the madness of the carver leapt from

2

the unfeeling rock to assault the sanity of all who gazed upon them. Veritas shuddered in the frigid, musty air.

Between the party and the towering monolith was rank upon rank of open caskets laid out upon the floor. Green-hued copper candelabra flanked the inlaid mosaic that led to the looming dais. The men hesitated to enter the chamber, fanning out around the doorway. Only the barbarian Halvar, seeming unimpressed, strode forward:

'Long dead,' he growled, spitting into the nearest coffin, frowning down at the dust-coated skeletal remains within. There was some nervous laughter from the guards, which echoed strangely for long seconds. 'There's more danger in my bone, than this lot!' He barked, leaning back hands on hips, crotch thrust forward suggestively, his large codpiece an affront to the dead.

Halvar's companion, the almost childlike leather-armoured gnome cut-purse, was already prowling the aisles.

'Treasure type fuck all.' he muttered to himself, moving toward the stone plinth, pale eyes flicking around warily.

Alfric, bearded and handsome, exuding an aura of natural authority, strode resolutely past the nervous men. His silvered ancestral plate mail gleamed in the flickering torchlight; soft echoes bounced from the strange, curved walls. With the reassuring tones of one bred to command, he ordered the men to spread out and search the dusty room.

'We're here to eradicate evil, men. We've cleared these caves of kobolds, but there may still be a troll. Whatever this,

place... is, it must be purified and cleansed. Nothing must be allowed to threaten our villages. The people depend upon us.'

As the men, emboldened by Alfric's words, spread out around the foreboding room, Veritas only had eyes for the hideously carved entity at the centre of this bizarre hollow. Hesitating only briefly, imploring Thea to give him courage, he moved along the exquisite inlaid mosaic pathway. Details hitherto obscured now stood out. The inlaid patterns of the aisle were curiously free of dust. Filigree of gold and silver highlighted scenes of hunting. Men in strange armour, with long spears and dark shields, strode through stylised forests and jungles. The artwork was masterful, yet curiously alien. He struggled to comprehend how this came to be here, in the heart of a remote mountain cavern.

Raising his eyes to again view the approaching platform, Veritas thought he could feel something emanating from the hulking form. Anything here must be aeons old, for the armour in the relief was of a style that the Priest could not place. It did not look like a form or pattern of the kingdoms that he was familiar with – yet the recumbent figures in the arrayed coffins certainly had been men. In his youth, he had adventured widely, and yet the whorls and serpentine carvings on the massive basalt block were utterly unfamiliar to him.

What was it, a bier? A sarcophagus? Of whom... and why would it be locked away in this starless grotto?

Circling to peruse the monolith, Veritas found the backside inlaid with marvellous deep purple gems! He gasped aloud, unable to contain himself, for this was wealth indeed. The diamond-cut jewels formed a stylised eye, maybe six hands across.

4

Set deep into the hard black stone of the dais, level with the Priest's breastbone, the winking gems scattered the light of his burning torch, refracting shifting patterns of lavender across his viridian robes.

'Another door here!' rumbled the massive Northman appearing to his left. His arrival snapped Veritas of his almost hypnotic fascination with the ornamentation of the altar. Looking up, he regarded Halvar. The big man was head and shoulders taller than the priest and had already proved himself a fierce warrior against the scaly dogmen, for whom he seemed to reserve a particular hatred. Uncouth and crass perhaps, but truly a good companion in an hour of need, praise the Lady.

'Nice,' said a voice from around his knee. Clarence, the gnome thief, who was never far away when Halvar was around, was staring appraisingly at the adornment of the dais.

'Keeping this to yourself eh, mummerer?' he said sharply, glancing up at Veritas.

'My friend, not at all. We of the priesthood decry wealth and provide all as a tithe to our Lady and saviour, for us…'

'Ha! He was just fucking with you, Grandad!' boomed a laughing Halvar, slapping the old priest on the back so hard that he caromed forward into the basalt edifice.

'Be a shame to leave 'em behind though,' said Clarence, 'I've never seen their like, they're not amethysts… brighter and more beautiful. Worth a tumble or two I'd wager,' he said, kicking Halvar in the ankle. The man-mountain laughed again and swung a huge leg back at the gnome. Who simply

vanished. It was a trick that he had performed several times and it never ceased to disconcert Veritas. That thief could hide behind a candle flame, he was sure. He did not trust him at all.

Forcing a smile, Veritas pushed back from the dais. Under his hand, which he had used to steady himself against the centre of the ornate relief, something shifted. Quickly stepping back, he could see that one of the stones had receded into the black face of the altar.

'Look Halvar, this one moves it...'

Then the walls blazed red.

***

Veritas whimpered at the recollection. Shame burned in him for failing. Failing his Lord, failing his God and finally fleeing in terror. Summoning what had returned of his courage and realising that he must move or perish, the old priest levered himself up. Leaning on his staff whilst cradling the faltering torch, he moved on down the dank rock tunnel. Time trundled torpidly past as he plodded forward on aching legs.

Wait. Was that light ahead? Veritas froze, *it was!*

The Priest's spirits briefly lifted, peering into the crepuscular dark, he could make out what appeared to be a dim slice of illumination stealing from below what could only be a doorway. A doorway that closed off his escape. The priest retreated into the black, mind racing. He was trapped – no way forward, and no retreat. Veritas must choose and he would do what he always did when faced with unclear things, he would pray to his Lady.

If she was still listening.

Chapter 2

The verdigris encrusted candelabras that ran the length of the aisle blazed with vivid scarlet flames. A dry wind whipped the cloak and tabards of Alfric and his men at arms.

'What in the Nine Hells is this?' shouted Lord Alfric, his men backing towards the entrance of the bizarre chamber.

'The dead riiiiise!' screamed Jessen the guard captain, pointing a shaking hand at the onyx coffins. Hastily moving back around the looming plinth, Veritas beheld a scene out of a nightmare. Bloody light and sinister shadow duelled across the walls, as the hitherto inert skeletal figures jerkily rose from their ancient tombs, dust cascading from their bleached limbs. Time-tarnished bronze helmets shone russet, contrasting with the dread white abomination of these animated cadavers.

Scarlet flames danced from the candles as the living dead hefted heavy black blades from within their biers. Courage wavering, Alfric's men clustered around their armoured master. Then without a sound, powered by necromantic verses from an eldritch age, the crypt warriors lurched forward to attack. Sparks rang as steel blades met ancient iron edges, living met dead and blood-spattered the aisle. Men used to fighting opponents of flesh withered as their blows did not slow their soulless enemies.

Jessen, with a triumphant cry, thrust his long sword between the vacant ribs of the haunted warrior before him. His war cry died as the gaunt fiend, unslowed, sheathed its dark blade in Jessen's throat. Black blood foamed from pale lips, as Jessen's life bubbled forth across the tiles of the ancient pathway. The metallic tang of blood filled the stagnant air.

To the shriek of swords on shields and the organic thunk of blades on flesh, the struggle surged back and forth between the ancient caskets. Hairy arms and sweating brows fought in frenzy against the cold evil of the osseous champions. Alfric's rich baritone bawled an order above the clangs and screams of the desperate combat.

'To me men, to me!'

Guards thrust and parried, their swords flashing crimson in the candlelight, whilst the emaciated warriors fought on in disquieting quietude.

Behind the altar and initially separated from the main group, Halvar burst upon the rear of the undead with barbaric ferocity. His hackles up, the mighty Northron reacted to the supernatural evil with the ferocity of the wild; born as he was beyond the veil of lies that civilisation constructs to hide from the terrors of the night. Hatred burned in Halvar's azure eyes, his enormous double-headed axe flashed scarlet, crushing the spine of the nearest cadaver and sending it flying in twain to splinter against the black stone walls. Leaping forward to engage the next of the fiends, he was a whirlwind of razor-edged destruction.

Veritas, hitherto frozen by this scene of terror, was jolted into action by the instant violence of the gigantic warrior. He stepped forward, right hand held aloft, summoning the power of his divine patron.

'Begone foul abominations!'

Veritas cried, voice finding courage and timbre as he raised his holy signet ring. Blessed by the Archbishop himself in the font of the Goddess Thea, it had never failed. Blinding ethereal light poured forth from emeralds set in the platinum band; the smell of cornfields and the warmth of a harvest sun radiated out, buoying them all. Veritas could feel his Lady's embrace, Her caress soothed him, Her love buoying him, Her power his to command.

The skeletal fiends turned to the rays as if struck, raising blanched bone arms to ward against the holy luminosity. To no effect. Purged by the Cleric's invoked emanation, wisps of vapour boiled forth as each skeleton began to crumble! Some tried clambering back into the wooden biers upon which they had lain for unknowable ages. But the scintillations seared and pursued them, mercilessly disintegrating the undead antagonists, until in moments they were gone; nothing but dust motes and ash yet lingering in the stagnant air.

Where before there had been frantic, urgent combat – now there was just the panting of the living and the silence of the dead. Alfric moved quickly to his fallen men. From the squad of keep guards that had accompanied him on this noble expedition, the fates had cursed four to an early grave.

Chainmail clinked as he knelt by Jessen's body; crimson blood still oozed from the guards' ruined throat. Alfric swore under his breath, another good man lost to the evil of this cursed mountain.

'Priest, hasten to me. I fear that the good captain is with our Lady now, blessed be his passage, but perhaps you can assist the others.'

10

Veritas hurried out from behind the basalt dais, tightly clasping the scuffed leather backpack which contained the unguents, potions and liniments that he had acquired through many years of adventuring and careful experimentation. As he pushed past the bulk of the scale mail clad Halvar, a massive hand thrust him backwards.

'What, I must…' he quavered.

'Why do the candles still burn?' hissed the hulking Northman, steel axe held to his chest, braided beard bristling. 'Something's not right here, I sense… witchery!'

'No, no, I'm sure…'

He was cut off as an alien, ear-splitting scream rent the air, descending from beyond the audible to assail their senses with apocalyptic wrath. Veritas stumbled to his knees, hands clamped over his bleeding ears, unable to think or act for the shattering, bone-piercing noise that assaulted them. On and on it pulsed; he could see Halvar's lips moving. Alfric was on his feet in front of the remaining sage hauberk guardsmen. He too was bawling something, face frantic, Veritas tried desperately to comprehend but could make out nothing through the ululating, furious caterwauling.

As quickly as the wall of sound had burst upon them, silence fell like a guillotine. Veritas could see the guards tentatively removing calloused hands from their ears, fearful of a resumption of the dreadful scream. Seconds dripped past, thick like molasses, and then blackness fell. The angry light of the unearthly candles winked out, leaving just the sputtering glow of the guards' torches.

Instantly the hair on Veritas' neck rose. Shadows seemed to expand and choke the remaining glow as, pale green and translucent, an ornately dressed female figure stepped forth from the slick basalt face of the grim sarcophagus.

The statuesque shade wore a pearlescent gown of stunning intricacy, and a jewel-encrusted tiara adorned the crown of her braided hair. Unnameable horror seemed to tear at the soul of the priest, as the blasphemous spectre turned her loathsome gaze upon him. The shocking beauty was made more terrible by the vacant eye sockets, which gaped empty and depthless in the angelic face.

Veritas' stomach churned as the undead terror gripped him. Hypnotised with an impotent mania he could only stare as the malignant manes floated forth. The apparition swept towards the two closest guards, phosphorescent fingers flickering forth to caress each stubbled cheek... and with a charnel sigh, they collapsed into inky dust before his eyes!

A resounding shout seemed to restart time in the claustrophobic amphitheatre. The ghastly paralysis that saw civilised men quail, had poured molten brass into the veins of the horn helmed Northman. Ancient terrors sparked simmering violence in him – the bestial rage of the cornered animal fired his adrenalized body into action. The massive axe blurred through the air, the primordial dread of this nightmare spirit lending strength to his mighty thews.

Yet the blade met no resistance! The figure parted like smoke, and the huge warrior crashed through the shade and into the onyx coffins beyond. Halvar staggered, steel blade striking sparks from the ebon floor. Thrown off balance by the violence of his blow, the warrior struggled to regain his fighting stance.

Ignoring the impotent strike, the shade bore down on Alfric, like a lover rushing to her swain.

*   'Stayyyy witthh meee….' The voice lanced into Veritas' mind, a sibilant whisper like a banshee's breath.*

*   Alfric moved slowly, far too slowly. He raised his sage crested shield, muscle memory thrusting it before him to slam his opponent back and off-balance. A life of tourney and adventure had steeped the great Lord in war. Wild beasts and varied heroes had fallen before his deadly blade, but this spectral witch was beyond his ken. A bone-deep chill embraced him, as the unearthly shade flowed through his defence. Shield, armour, flesh and blood were no barrier against such soulless assault.*

*   Reeling from the phantasmal force the nobleman buckled, pitching forward, his left hand thrust out, right refusing to drop his gold-hilted sword of office.   Dread lined the face Alfric turned to Veritas, swarthy skin pale in the torchlight.*
*   The priest again raised his consecrated ring, his talisman against evil. His master's hour of need implored!*

*   'My Lady!' he the band held forth, reaching deep within.*

Emptiness.

No light. No sanctity. No power.

No deliverance.

*   Staggered, feeling every day of his five decades of life, the cleric whimpered. Always, always She was there for him… his saviour, the vocation of his entire life. How could this be? In*

13

disbelieving horror, he looked at the platinum circle that had not left his hand since placed there a score of years ago. It remained dim.

With a sense of impotent calamity, the holy man looked back to his Lord and master. Alfric was on his knees, hand-held toward Veritas as he had for communion every sabbath for as long as the old man could recall.

The sinister swaying shade loomed behind Alfric. The air was deathly still, yet her blue-white tresses flowed as if blown in a fierce wind. With crawling horror, Veritas' eyes met the vacant sockets of the spectre. The spirit's lips twitched, and then the fiend smiled at him!

With great delicacy and an execrable simulacrum of tenderness, the pallid princess pushed a pale hand smoothly through Alfric's breastplate, the burnished steel proving porous as tissue.

Veritas screamed.

Alfric's face dissolved into cascading, shimmering dust.

Mind swamped with the tides of nightmare; the old man fled. With never a background glance, arms pumping, mouth slack, he pelted into the darkness.

Chapter 3

Veritas sat huddled in the black. For how long he had hunched there was not clear. The torch had gone cold some time ago and the clammy chill of this deep dungeon corridor had entered his soul. He could do nothing but endlessly recall the scenes of the disaster, over and over again. Teetering on the brink of a despair he would never emerge from, Veritas realised he was listening to the low rumble of the distant thunder. Or perhaps an underground river…

He shifted position on the packed earth floor, head held on one side. Now that he concentrated on it, the prelate realised with alarm that it was getting louder, gaining strength.

Wait, what, but...?

The old priest shuddered at the thought of what might emerge from the midnight passages that lay behind. Forcing his aching limbs to function, Veritas clambered upright. Clearer now, he could hear…it sounded like… running feet… but the footfalls were impossibly fast. The echoes here made guessing distance hard, but before he could make any rudimentary preparation, the enormous form of the barbarian Halvar tore around the corner of the passageway and bowled him over. The big man moved with incredible speed, but skidded to a halt just as swiftly, towering over the sprawling Veritas.

'Afternoon, Preacher,' he boomed, 'what are you doing on your arse?'

Clarence moved away, leaving Halvar to explain the details of their escape from the spectral crypt. He wanted to examine the door that the priest had mentioned. It was the only new thing gleaned from the garbled monologue that Veritas had just concluded. The thief judged the bloodshot-eyed priest as now too crazed to be a reliable witness, so he would make a professional assessment of this new obstruction.

He could use a few minutes to think anyway. The shattering of the party by the ghost, or whatever it had been, had radically changed his hopes for the outcome of this adventure. Placing his feet precisely, using his natural infravision to pick out stones or anything else that might give him away, he ghosted up the corridor. Born dextrous, Clarence had studied hard at the Guild. Shadows and silence were a thief's best weapon said Master Bellof, and he was right.

Deep gnomes, for that he was, were blessed with the ability to see heat, and also to see in the ultraviolet. The latter was not much use to him here, the hulking mass of stone above them filtered out most of the blue spectrum. Still, he could see well enough that he needed no torch.

Alfric had regularly complained that the little thief never seemed around, but that was merely due to ensuring that he was outside the circle of light created by the group. The torches deepened the darkness and announced their arrival with fool's flame.

Then there was his *other* emerging skillset, but he had not mentioned that. Only Halvar knew and he was not about to explain a concept like psionics to anyone. Clarence grinned in the darkness as he thought briefly of Halvar. He had never met anyone quite as… well, stupid.

Maybe simple was a better term, simple like a smile, simple like a fist. It made many people underestimate him, usually to their physical cost. For neither had he ever met anyone as immensely, peerlessly strong as the Northman. He was a force of nature. Devastating in combat, with huge self-confidence paired with an uncanny ability to change a situation with the action least expected. In their short time together, Clarence had grown fond of the big oaf.

Gnome society was Halvar's complete opposite; stuffy, staid, stolid. Risk-averse and endlessly boring, Clarence had come to hate his brothers and sisters of the deep. Their unthinking conservatism, their niggardly pettiness, the mistrust of all 'Bigs'. Ninety years before you reached adulthood and could own property, no magic and no traders. No damned excitement!

Gnomes were long-lived that was true, the greybeards could reach more than five hundred years old and still be quite active. Active but dull. He had heard that some of the other tribes were less restrictive.

The day the clan elders had summoned Clarence to pay penance for teaching himself how to throw daggers was the day he had filled his pack and walked.

All knew the path: The Dawn Way. The weaving track to the uplands and the human realms. It was *the cursed road*, *the God-spurned way*, *the*… blah blah blah. Wrinkled-faced clan elders told scare stories to the gnome children, pathetically huddled around crackling dung fires. Stories of mistrust, betrayal, feckless humans and the abusive behaviour of all the other 'mongrel' races.

It was true that life up in the light was very different, Clarence had to wear dark glasses above ground, but for all the inconvenience and culture shock, he had not regretted leaving for a moment.

As for Biggers, well they did not come much more so than Halvar, who at six foot ten inches was over twice the gnome's height. Clarence had first met the barbarian warrior holding forth in a tavern about his skill at arms, his skill with women, and his skill at cards. All whilst two fools at the table were sharping him. Halvar had not noticed and probably never would have if Clarence had not strategically nudged one of the card smith's hands. After the ensuing melee and subsequent flight from the bill for barroom damages, they had hit it off straight away.

Clarence lurked in the shadows, ensuring that nobody could con the crazy wildman and Halvar... well, he did his thing. Their partnership had proven remarkably successful in the months since that fateful day. Plus of course, he was having more fun than he ever had in all the decades in the Underdark.

This time though, Clarence was scared. They had hired on to this expedition to clear out the mountain cave system near Alfric's home, simply and swiftly. Peasants of the Duchy being raided by Kobolds could not be tolerated, not within spitting distance of the Lord's keep. A poor reward was to be expected when dealing with dogmen, that was true, but they had agreed to a full half share of any treasure found, plus the upfront gold pieces. He was glad of that dispensation now, only a fool would return to the Duke given the death of his only son. The caves had been tangled and far deeper than suspected, and now the disaster of the black crypt had probably made the two of them wanted men for a dozen days ride in all directions. The old boy Manfred was not a forgiving ruler: he would want someone to suffer for this.

What in the Nine Hells had been going on with that shit anyway? Some sort of undead mausoleum to a forgotten sorceress... Is fucking Asmodeus down here too?

Clarence shuddered. If Halvar had not smashed the corridor ceiling down with his axe as they fled, their budding partnership might have ended right there. It did make one thing very clear though, there was no way out now but onwards, or as he sensed, downwards.

Slipping through the fathomless black, Clarence approached the doorway. Dust and cobwebs crusted this side of the portal, a large rat startled by his stealthy approach pressed itself into a crack in the wall, ruby eyes twinkling.

A dim sliver of light crept out from beneath the elderly banded iron door, which Clarence judged not to be from a fire or torchlight. If experience of the deep told him anything, this was some sort of fungal luminosity. There were many types of glowing mushrooms and other mycelium down here, and many a deep creature that fed on them.

With all the pressure of an autumn leaf falling, Clarence pressed his ear to the wood and held his breath.

Silence.

Patiently, he waited and did his best to focus. At the very limits of his perception, he thought he could perceive distant grunting. Perhaps snoring? Clarence was not sure, but if forced to wager he would guess it was from more than one source.

Listening at doors was another skill the guild trained in, but whilst he had practised extensively, it was a tricky thing to master. How do you listen better?

'Slow the heart rate, clear the mind, focus on your surroundings.'

Well and good, but the climbing and sneaking were more his metiers. After several minutes, with nothing further gleaned, Clarence padded back to his companions.

In the dim light of the sole torch, Veritas sat slumped against the stone passage wall. The elderly priest's head sagged between his shoulders, and he was shivering. Halvar was striding back and forth before him, regaling him with the tale of their escape from the earlier encounter.

'Yeah, so then Alfric came back to life controlled by the witch thing,' said Halvar, as Clarence approached.

Veritas' head snapped up and shadows played across his haggard face.

'What did you say?' croaked the old man, voice cracking. His bloodshot eyes flicked back and forth from Halvar's giant form to the diminutive gnome.

'Like I said, he got up again all green and see-through, and started after us,' said Halvar. 'Me and

Clarence legged it then, and I used this to smash down the ceiling.' Halvar patted his enormous double-headed axe fondly before gesticulating violently with it at the corridor roof, beard braids swinging. Veritas' face turned to Clarence, mania straining his gaunt features.

'Is that true?' he asked, shakily getting to his feet.

'Umm, what's that?' said the gnome, knowing full well what was meant, but unsure how to deal with this. The Cleric had the air of a man pushed beyond his wits.

'Halvar said that Alfric was raised as a ghost,' he said, in halting tones '...by the Spectre…that's, that's not true, is it?'

Clarence took a moment to examine the features of the elderly Cleric. He had not been planning to mention that fact. Certainly not now that he had seen the man's skittish behaviour. The dark affected humans in odd ways and it was not surprising that the old man was on edge after the disaster in the crypt. His Lord and master, whom he had cared for since Alfric was born, was dead. That was enough to shake anyone.

Clarence had quite liked Alfric, certainly he had not affected any of the usual xenophobic attitudes encountered elsewhere. Most men in power seemed either dismissive at best, or more often downright supremacist towards other species. Alfric had been decent to him. More surprising really, given that Clarence had heard rumours that the old Duke was nothing of the sort.

'Does it matter?' he said, trying to squeeze as much compassion as he could into his words, 'They're all dead Veritas,' he added quietly, 'there's nothing to be done about that now.'

'Tell me!' shrieked the Cleric, his usually mild voice echoing back and forth from the cold rock. Clarence's eyes flashed urgently down the passage towards the doorway. It was more than fifty yards, but he could see its blue outline at the limits of his infravision. Sound travelled farther in tight spaces, and he did not like the prospect of being trapped in here by whatever was beyond. He made frantic motions with his hands to encourage the man to lower his voice.

'Answer me!' screamed the priest, 'I'll not be responsible for leaving that boy to eternal evil!' Spittle flew from his lips, as his dust-rimed emerald robes flapped beneath windmilling arms. Shaking hands reached for the gnome, as Veritas tried to clutch at his shoulders.

'Quiet!' hissed Clarence, skipping out of reach. 'Hush, Priest, you forget where we are. There is still danger here.'

Halvar growled deep in his throat, eyeing the blackness ahead. Clarence's concern set the hulking warrior on edge. Unable to lay hands on the thief, Veritas pawed instead at Halvar's mailed chest, torchlight reflected from his wide staring eyes.

'We must go back, we must! We must purify, must raise them. A consecration…' He gibbered, hands batting

22

at the barbarian's broad breast. 'You understand, don't you Halvar? I won't leave HIM!'

'Easy, Preach, we can't get back that way,' interrupted the bearded Northman, gently fending off his feeble flailing.

Suddenly, a bark echoed down the passageway, followed by a mighty thump. The door shook as if struck by a battering ram, ancient hinges buckling from the force. All eyes turned to stare, although neither human could see that far in the dim light.

Clarence cursed silently, he recognised that sound and this was the worst place to face an enemy like *them*.

With a reverberating crunch, the iron banded door split full length and flew apart, swinging shattered from a single hinge. Beyond, as only the gnome could see, the way was blocked by two enormous shapes, nine feet tall with thin spindly arms ending in large claw-tipped hands. Legs bowed below large bellies, the creatures had the mottled colouring and fang-filled skulls manifesting what could only be...

'Trolls!' hissed Clarence.

The newcomers started swiftly up the way towards the trapped party. Everyone knew trolls. Unstoppable nightmares of carnivorous appetite, they could and would eat anything. Halvar spat and raised his axe.

Whirling towards the distant crash, the crazed Cleric sprang forward and jerked a dagger from his belt.

'My boy, Alfric!' he yelled, 'I'm coomiinnnnggg....'

Lank hair flying Veritas screamed incoherently and sprinted away from his companions towards the distant menace. His leather sandals slapped against the lichen-coated earth, emerald robes trailing behind him as cometlike he receded into the dark. Halvar looked confusedly down at his companion,

'What the fuck?'

If the priest's mind was gone, Clarence's was racing. There was no way out behind them he knew, and now it seemed unlikely there was much ahead. Trolls were one of the most feared creatures of the wilds, their claws and teeth could rip through steel, and they shrugged off wounds that would stop a storm giant. Their flesh and bone could knit back together almost any injury, and swiftly, it was terrifying to behold. Only with preparation could they be overcome. Acid and fire were the secrets, otherwise, those putrid green bastards would never stop coming at you. Chop them up into little bits all you like, turn your back and a couple of minutes later they were back and angrier than ever.

The party had known there might be a troll when they set off on this adventure, and so had brought oil flasks with them.

Preparation was everything... so much for that.

Turning to look up at Halvar, who was implacably watching Veritas' torch recede towards the approaching horrors, Clarence said:

24

'Halv, the only way out of this mountain is through those trolls. Remember their bloody regeneration though and don't stop for anything!'

The big man grunted and leant down. Shifting his short sword to lie flatter across his back, Clarence leapt for the same position on the muscular shoulders that he had clung to during their earlier flight. Throwing his left arm around the huge neck, and wedging his feet into the Northman's weapon backstrap, he hung on. Unhindered by the additional weight and hefting his mighty axe, the barbarian accelerated down the dingy passageway.

One thing that nobody in the party had known was that the huge warrior had an edge, other than that of his prodigious strength. Halvar did not trust magic, like all barbarians he was both in awe of, and belligerently against magic in all its forms. However, on a recent pillaging, the pair had come across an amazing thing. A pair of boots, ostentatious, gauche even, in black leather with flaming horses picked out with crimson and gold thread.

'*Boots of Speed*,' the Sage had called them when they had visited upon returning to the city.

'Flashy,' Halvar said admiringly pulling them on, before strutting back and forth in front of the Sage's ornate mirror.

'Mine.' he had stated, and that was that.

Deep down, Clarence suspected that the big man knew they were enchanted. However, he had allowed himself to be 'persuaded' to keep them after a demonstration of what they could do. For Halvar could now run as fast as a galloping horse. It had saved the two of them on more than one occasion and provided a significant surprise factor in many combat encounters. Clarence wedged himself tighter into position as the steel trap muscles of the barbarian accelerated at the fanged fury that was meantime rushing towards them.

Ahead Veritas, robes flapping and an ululating scream issuing from his lips, charged the confused-looking trolls. Mottled green and tan, with pointed ears and dark wiry hair on their elongated skulls, the tall, emaciated figures were hurrying forward.   Unsure how this yelling figure had come to be in this closed-off passageway, the beasts were not about to turn down free food. Grinning, the leading troll flung razor-clawed arms wide across the path of the sprinting man. Dull grey drool dripping from blackened maw, it sprang at the approaching Cleric.

The old man swung his dagger high and brought it down with fanatical fury at the large shape blocking his way. The blade sliced along the upraised forearm, leaving a deep cut that oozed thick green ichor. The troll grunted but unslowed swung its long right arm at the man's midsection. Veritas' headlong flight left no room for evasion, yet even in his madness he attempted to weave aside, but the confined space left no room for nuance. The troll's four-inch claws raked across his robe-clad stomach tearing him open. Dark blood and pulsing mauve entrails flew from the hideous wound to slap, wet and steaming, onto the cold tunnel wall. The priest screamed and was thrown like a rag doll by the savagery of the blow, smashed into the frigid stonework.

Before he could make another sound, both of the slavering trolls were upon him. The first eagerly pushed its hand into the gaping rent in the old man's bloody robes, twisting its claws in his vital organs. Veritas' last sight was of the second beast's hideous jaws thrown wide, pulling him up by his hair before its yellow fangs crunched into his skull.

At incredible speed, Halvar leapt the last twenty feet with a mighty spring. The massive axe blurred in a wide sweep to connect with the foremost troll. The beast tried to raise a hairy arm in defence, but being distracted by having already started to consume the corpse at its feet, it was far too slow.

The steel blade entered the bloated body through the collar bone on the right side of its bat-eared head and sank deep into the corpulent belly. The savagery of the blow threw the beast aside, and gore fountained through the air, the troll nearly torn in half by the sheer force. Crashing past its feasting companion, it rolled back across the pathway, hot bilious blood spattering across the grime of the passage floor.

The second troll rushed forward, gap-toothed maw snarling at the flying barbarian. Closing, it attempted to grapple and crush its foe in a sinuously strong grip. Halvar was the mightiest amongst his wild people but knew enough not to try and wrestle a hill troll.

The beast ducked left with amazing speed, dodging a short-bladed dagger hurled by Clarence. The thief's perch was not good for accuracy, but the distraction proved enough. The troll had not allowed for the tremendous speed of the huge Northman, who without time to pull back his axe for another swing, simply levelled it and used the pointed tip as a spear.

The six-inch point lanced between the monster's ribs and the peerless muscle power of the charging barbarian lifted the enormous creature off its feet. The combination of huge strength and magical speed carried it on the end of the axe for a dozen paces before man and troll slammed past the hanging, ruined doorway and into the cave beyond.

Halvar's careering course crashed across the filthy cave beyond until the slavering troll was pinned to the opposite wall. In the near darkness of the new space, the mighty warrior paused. The torch that the late priest had carried was slowing spitting out on the floor of the corridor behind, and this room contained no light source other than the pale, sickly phosphorescence of the lichen that matted the walls. In this sinister incandescence, he could see barely ten paces into the gloom. Not that he was looking, his attention was entirely focused on the thrashings of the snarling menace he had temporarily fixed to the cavern wall.

Stepping back, and with an instinct to incapacitate this abhorrent creature, he ripped the axe point free of the bony breast and swept it down at the bandy legs.

The troll howled as the curved steel ripped through its left leg, bone and sinew sliced apart by the vicious short-arm chop. Jaws champed open and closed, mouth-frothing, green blood pumping from the hideous wound. The long arms reached for him, curved onyx claws skittering on scale armour, but found no purchase. Then the wounded troll collapsed sideways, to sprawl on the detritus-strewn floor.

Clarence, from his rocking perch, had been casting his eyes around the newly visible cavern. It stretched away to left and right, as far as his night vision could reach. However, most pressingly, he could see three more of the savage monstrosities urgently clambering to their taloned feet. Alerted by the cries of combat, they rushed towards where Halvar stood. Snatching a glance over his shoulder, he could make out the near-dissected troll crawling towards them, dragging its shattered body along with one good arm. The hideous, puss-green flesh of the gaping wound had already begun to knit back together.

'Left, run left!' Clarence yelled, being sure to shout into that ear so the big man did not confuse his meaning. 'Go, go, go! There are more of them!'

Halvar cannily kicked the recumbent troll's severed leg away; it cartwheeled towards the newly alerted monsters, blood trailing from the dismembered stump. Whirling out of the reach of the nearest claws he sprinted into the blackness. The remaining trolls howled and ran after him, heads held low, bodies stooped as if to smell his trail in the inky black.

Halvar ran and ran, trusting to the paltry light of the fungus and Clarence's urgings. Their bowlegs were not designed for sprinting, but by using their arms like gorillas, the trolls were able to knuckle along at considerable speed.

A normal man would undoubtedly have been brought down within the first dozen yards, but the speeding warrior soon began to hear their howls of rage recede. There could be no let-up though, for they had passed no side passages or forks at which they could hope to shake the deadly pack. Down and down the cave continued. It seemed more natural than the passageway in which they had lost their companion, less constructed. Clarence could make out other creatures of the black as they pelted by, a giant centipede the size of a dachshund glowed pinkly in his night sight. Some rats flashed past, and then what may have been a large spider in a recess above a collapsed area of the cave wall. Leaning down he said,

'You, ok?'

'Piece of Piss!' said the big man, seemingly not even sweating from his exertions. He ran carrying his enormous axe before him as if it weighed nothing. No small accomplishment, as the gnome could attest to. Clarence was strong for his size, but he could barely *lift* the ridiculously oversized thing.

The cave narrowed of a sudden, the ceiling moving to within a few feet of the Northman's horned helmet. The walls too closed in, and suddenly they were back in what appeared more like a corridor. The walls were deeply embedded with baroque whirls and there were channels and pits carved into the floor and ceiling. Clarence could no longer hear any pursuit.

A moment later, at the limits of his vision, he saw a broad doorway blocking their path. It stood eight feet high and four across.

'Halvar, slow up my friend, there's a door ahead.'

Halvar, whose blood was still afire from the recent combat, shouted back:

'I'll charge it down!' and lowered his shoulder, picking up speed.

'What!? No, Halvar stop we're clear!'

'It's fine!' he boomed in reply and before Clarence could say another word, slammed into the door with unstoppable force. There was a splintering crash as mail-clad barbarian met aged wooden portal; the thick timbers rotten with years splintered asunder.

The room beyond had walls, but no floor! In an instant the two were plunging through space, shards of shattered oak plummeting with them as they tumbled into the soot-black depths of the pit.

Chapter 4

* One week earlier *

Jimkin bustled around behind the long beechwood bar, replacing the mead barrels that had been emptied last evening. Duchy-crested shields, horse tack and other war memorabilia adorned the dark wood walls of the inn. His heavy moustache bristled as he rolled the last barrel into its spigot housing. It had certainly been a rowdy night, lots of people in town for the Duke's tournament, strange folk too. He had been landlord of 'The Basket' for near on twenty years now since his old Ma had passed away, and he had never seen the like of it. They had set up jousting lanes on the green, and a melee square by the arches, people had come from all over the shire to try their hand. Rangers and other quarrelers at the archery, the nobles of nearby fiefdoms trouped in for the lancing, and of course, anyone could enter the melee.

Everybody loved a public holiday and m'Lord Alfric's squire had even bought the first ten casks for the beer tents. There had been bunting strung from the rooftops and all manner of stalls and entertainments. Hog roasts, a ducking stool, artisans selling their wares, cock fights and they had even caught a bugbear to bait. Big ugly bugger, he had put up a good fight before the guard captain had swaggered in to finish him off. Jessen knew how to play to the crowd, holding up the hideous head to scare the screaming kids.

Good times! He thought smiling.

Jimkin had seen his first high elf of the season, no less than four of them on beautiful white horses, with mirror-finish *ribbon traces and electrum stirrups. They had not gotten involved in anything of course. Snooty buggers by all accounts, but he took folk as he found, and their gold paid for his wine the same as anyone else's. Spring must be here though, as it was said they would not leave their woods till the blossom came.*

This morning he was up early, as usual, to swill down the privies and clean up the bar. Not too many breakages this time, which was unusual after a festival. Mind you with all the gentry about and the guardsmen in residence, it was a brave man who decided to cut up rough. The stocks were well greased, and nobody wanted to be the example.

The smell of chitterlings, bacon and eggs sizzling wafted through from the kitchen to the bar and set his rotund stomach to rumbling. He had eaten already of course, but there was usually time for a second snack around ten. Jimkin tamped down his hunger for now, as he loaded up the tray that Cook brought through the hatch and carefully carried it into the back of the inn. Here, m'Lord Alfric was at this moment finalising his preparations for the purging of the hills.

There had been raids in these lands for some time now, dogmen and other beasts, so the young master had brought a troop of his best. They looked mighty impressive in the Ducal regalia. All shiny breastplates and sage hauberks, with the lazy griffon on there. "Couchant" he had been told was the correct term. Apparently, it was foreign for lying down. It did look like it was asleep though, and so everyone called them The Snoozers.

Jimkin smiled again as he deftly negotiated the swing doors without spilling the coffee on the tray.

'So, I trust everyone is prepped and ready?' said a voice he recognised as Lord Alfric.

'Aye sir, we've a full squad, and the other specialists are staying in this inn,' came the reply 'but, my Lord, would we not be better waiting for the main body to arrive two days hence?'

'We dare not, Jessen, the raids are daily now. I'll not see one more of our people taken or lose another damned wagon, not if I can do anything to stop it. The second group will follow directly after us.'

'Understood, Sir.'

'Good man. Fetch the others then, we will repast and then head out. This is not meant to be a lengthy excursion, and Father says better not waste much time.' Catching sight of the large form of the publican, he said.

'Ah, Mr Jimkin. Thank you.' Alfric sat down at the map-strewn board, swiftly clearing space and setting about the heaped breakfast tray.

'Just the man' said the dark-haired young Captain, moving around the large oak table and clapping a hand on Jimkin's shoulder. 'We'll be leaving within the hour' he said, as they both returned to the barroom. 'Are the horses ready, and the carriages?'

'Yessir, the coachman and the boy are in the stables now loading up.'

'Splendid, and what about Brandt, our mighty melee mauler?' said Jessen laughing. 'Not a scratch after that series of bouts. He's certainly earned his place on this little expedition.'

Jimkin rubbed his double chin with concern.

'Ah.' he replied brow wrinkling in the dappled light streaming through the grand bar window. He had been hoping against hope that the fiery fighter would be down by now. Unfortunately for all concerned, Brandt had been mighty full of himself in the bar last night. After which there had been that 'incident' with the massive Northman.

'I'll go and fetch him,' he said and scurried towards the stairwell.

Jimkin thought back to the crowded bar last night as he huffed his way up the broad, red-carpeted stairs. Brandt was a barrel-chested southerner, sun-bronzed from campaigning amongst the Tulars in the broad deserts beyond the inland sea. Truly a mighty warrior, and strong as a mountain bear. The melee champion was instantly the centre of attention upon arrival, still clad in the grime-encrusted hauberk he had worn beneath his chainmail.

Men and women clustered around his table convivially, to a background of excited chatter and the odd song. They were enthralled with his tales of combat and braggadocio. Initially enthralled that is. Brandt had been amiable and voluble. However, after several beers, he had begun holding forth about the lack of a challenge received in the square that afternoon. Whilst in truth, he had completely dominated the event, the proud people were a little affronted by this new boast. The firelight reflected from the brass studs in his leather breeches as he laughed,

'None of you ninnies were able to even scratch me, what a pathetic effort,' he barked to mutters and a few laughs. 'This beer isn't as good as our desert wines either.' He regarded the

amber fluid swirling in his tall glass. 'Ah well, you've got me
here to save the day, haven't you? Show you how it's done.'

Jimkin knocked politely on the thick mahogany panel
adorning the Emperor's Suite door, recalling what had happened
next. In the corner of the room, nursing his foaming ale had been
another giant of a man. Pale-skinned and with a twin-forked
beard, the brooding warrior arrived too late for the day's
festivities. For a while, he had seemed content to drown his
frustrations in endless beers, but he now barged through the
throng that had gathered around the man of the hour.

The giant swaggered up to Brandt, people clearing a path
before him. The smile was cheerful, but the eyes were burning
with the intensity of a banked furnace.

'Listen up, Fatty!' He exclaimed in a scathing tone,
frowning and poking the southern man in his broad chest. 'I am
Halvar T Barbarian, a NORTH MAN!' He glanced around at
the townsfolk whom he towered over, grinning. 'And you,' he
continued, voice dripping with insolence, 'are a soft southern
bitch!'

There were loud gasps from the crowd. The newcomer
sat down opposite Brandt with one brawny arm, corded with
muscle, raised for the classic test of strength, the arm wrestle.

'I challenge you...'

Brandt seemed a little flustered at being riposted quite
like this, but his bullish self-confidence was never far away. He
sat down on the oak bench, raising his huge arm and scoffed:

'Don't you need Mummy's permission first, Boy?'

In the bright glow of the firelight, the two mighty hands clasped... Immediately, the whipcrack muscles of the wildman slammed Brandt's hand to the tabletop with a mighty crash. Glasses leapt along the trestle table and the moustachioed Southerner was thrown to one side with stunning force.

Halvar stood up and roared, arms aloft. In his left hand, he yet held the foaming tankard that the crowd now saw he had not set aside. They cheered and laughed as, emboldened, the huge figure stood on the bench and flexed his muscles ostentatiously towards a gaggle of the festival-dressed town girls near the door.

'The NORRRRTH, The NORRRRTH!' he bellowed.

A furious Brandt shoved aside the crowded onlookers as he struggled to regain his feet.

'CHEAT!' He yelled, as the noise was replaced with a pregnant hush. 'Cheating Northerner!' he continued menacingly, staring at the gloating face of his opponent. 'You must wait for the signal to start.' Silence reigned until the huge warrior hissed a reply.

'What!? Did you say that to me?' eyes ablaze, he glared at Brandt.

'I wasn't ready. There are rules to this man's game, young imbecile.'

The grim, scale-clad barbarian waited, bubbling with anger, fists clenching and unclenching, scowling at the swarthy champion before him. Tense moments passed as the onlooker's

37

eyes flickered between the twin colossi. Calling out a cheat was not something easily forgiven.

'I demand satisfaction!' said Brandt, looking around with some returning ebullience he added magnanimously.

'I tell you what, I'll only fight you to first blood. I know there are rules about duelling during the festival, luckily for you.' Voice jeering, he added, 'Outside, Boy and I'll beat the cost of my drink out of your simpleton skin.'

Without reply, Halvar turned on his heel and stalked swiftly out through the half doors ahead of Brandt, into the brisk night air. The packed dirt road in front of the inn was well lit by the glowing embers of the bonfire on the green, and the many lanterns whose light pooled by bright doorways.

Patrons rushed out into the road, heads appeared at doors and windows, as the two men stood facing each other not eight feet apart, personifications of power.

'You go first, Fatso!' sneered Halvar, as Brandt raised his fists into the tight protective stance of the experienced boxer. He danced on the balls of his feet, moving with surprising grace for anyone who had not seen his earlier prowess, loose and agile. Alcohol had not slowed him at all it seemed. No doubt intending to show off his hand speed, he threw a couple of snapping jabs into the air well away from the hulking Northman.

'Scared yet?' he smirked.

'Missed!' roared Halvar, and springing forward like a panther, delivered a crushing, shattering kick to the melee champion's groin. There was a collective groan from the crowd, with a few high-pitched laughs. The big man crashed forward,

38

crumpling to one knee. His legs were shaking, and the skin on his neck had turned a mottled purple. Breath whistled between clenched teeth as he struggled not to fall. Pain seared into Brandt's guts; all sounds extinguished except pumping blood roaring in his ears. A shadow fell across him.

'You couldn't fight kittens' hissed Halvar. Pulling Brandt up by the hair in one massive fist, he brought his blonde head snapping down with devastating speed. The deafening crack as the skulls collided bounced back from surrounding alleys and distant buildings. Then the brawny man rocketed backwards, head lolling on his massive shoulders as he crashed into the inn steps. Splinters and dust billowed as Brandt rolled, coming to rest crumpled and broken against the stable doors.

'Easy!' said the barbarian before strutting back inside, still brandishing the frothing beer he had never relinquished. The crowd stared agog.

'Next barrel is on me, Barman!' he called to a resurgence of rowdy cheers, hoots, and hollers. The dazed drinkers followed, quickly clustering back into the warmth of the tavern in fine humour. The honour of the north was restored, and everyone was boisterously full of cheer.

Jimkin had later helped carry Brandt to the room he had won as the champion of the melee. The man had a lump the size of a swan's egg on his forehead. Jimkin felt a little bad for the hefty warrior, but not that bad. He had gone too far to expect real sympathy the tavern master thought. Plus, the drinking had picked up again afterwards. A fat purse for him, and a fine end to the festival.

As for cheating? Hmmph… well. Don't mess about with barbarians would've been his advice. There were different rules, out beyond civilisation and sometimes things got lost in translation. It was all good fun and banter until there was an angry tribe burning down your town in a blood feud.

Aye, all in all, best not to mess he thought.

Jimkin knocked a third time at the suite door and then finally entered the inn's plush main bedchamber. He hurried over to the figure slumped on the four-poster, feet soundless on the thick carpet. Brandt had not moved from where they had lain him last night, white sheets framing his enormous form. The beefy publican checked for a pulse, breathing a thankful sigh when he found one. He felt the man's brow; again, all seemed well. However, he could not wake the unconscious fighter no matter what he tried. After a few minutes of fruitless effort, he closed the door behind him and hurried back down the broad stairs.

'No sign of sleeping beauty?' said a small voice from behind the polished panelling of the bar. Jimkin turned and moving forward was now able to regard a small figure in leather, perched on a bar stool, yellow eyes gazing sharply up at him.

'Doesn't look like he's going to be ready for the Duke's mission, eh?' The strange individual continued to the amazement of the burly innkeeper. Jimkin's mouth was hanging open; he closed it.

'Are you a gnome?' he said, curious, for the small folk were rare in these parts.

'That's right, Chap. A gnome of many talents. Beginning with finding you a replacement for the comatose

braggart upstairs. Think you could make an introduction to Lord Alfric for me?'

The big man looked over the gnome's head to the back table, where Jessen and Alfric were deep in discussion.

'I err, well I…'

The diminutive figure smiled warmly at him.

'That's really appreciated, Friend, I'll certainly make it worth your while.'

Chapter 5

Clarence started awake at shouts and curses from somewhere above him. Aching horrendously down his battered left side, he spat blood.

Not again!

Trying to focus, Clarence realised he was sprawled against a crumbling stone wall at the bottom of a deep shaft. A thick resin coated him and the bed of sticks and detritus that he had landed in. Here and there he could see hints of metal, shining blue in his infravision.

Rolling over and trying to rise, he was of a sudden splashed down the side of his face and arms with hot, sticky fluid. As he reached up to wipe his eyes clear, Clarences fell amongst the debris. Attempting to stand once more, he tried to take in what was happening.

'Fuck you, Bastard!' came the unmistakable sound of Halvar yelling from somewhere above. Struggling in the goo, he cast his eyes upwards and beheld a scene out of a nightmare.

Stretching back and forth across the enormous shaft that rose into the darkness, were what Clarence now perceived to be the strands of a gigantic web. Threads and tendrils, some as thick as his arm, wove back and forth intertwining as far as he could see into the distant black.

Thirty feet above, the giant form of the barbarian was held fast in the main lattice. He was lashing out, arms whirring to fend off an enormous arachnid. Chitinous armour reflected the dim phosphorescent glow of the lichen-matted walls. Sturdy, spiked legs were attempting to throw ropes of diaphanous webbing around the desperately floundering man, as the beast hissed its fury.

From below, Clarence could not make out its full details even with his superior night vision. Shaking his head groggily, he pushed through what he now realised, with mounting terror, were bones that littered the floor of this gruesome lair. He pulled his foot free of a large rib cage which had been picked clean of tissue. Then, trying not to become entangled in a rotten backpack, he lurched his way over to the craggy rock wall.

The thick viscous liquid coating his left side, he now realised with a frisson of horror, was blood, but even his infravision could not tell if it was human or spider.

With all the urgency that he could muster, he began to climb the slick rock, hands feeling out the small protuberances and outgrowths in the dim light. His head throbbed and he felt sick from his earlier fall. Ringing in his mind were the words of old Bellof:

'You need to be able to do this in the dark boy, a mark will rarely leave the lights on!'

The Guild owned a modular hotel built in the heart of the city, to all intents and purposes looking like a drab tenement. Inside, however, it aped the finery of the upmarket establishments where the aristocracy spent thousands of gold pieces a night in the fashionable districts near the harbour. Everything could be changed. Walls slid back and forth on oiled rollers, furniture moved, pictures, passages, doors; secret and mundane. Gradings were held in the Conti; a contraction of the mocking nickname 'The Continental', as the dark north was rarely warm or varied. Besides this, it had no official moniker. All of this flashed back and forth in his addled brain, as he clambered within feet of the base of the clinging fronds.

Above him, the complex lattice shook violently as beast and man struggled back and forth. Hissing sibilant spits, expostulations and loud curses reverberated up and down the grim chamber. Suddenly a strained yell rose above the ruckus, Halvar crying out in evident agony.

'Come here!' roared Halvar, followed by a sickening crunch, and a glissando of warbling hissing. Halvar cursed again. The web shuddered and something rushed downwards just behind the climbing gnome.

Silence fell and the mesh swayed itself still. Reaching up, Clarence steadied himself on a cloyingly sticky web tendril, and arching his back, looked at the large outline of the recumbent man.

'Halvar, you ok?' No answering call came. 'Halvar!' he said loudly, already despairing.

'Hmm, what?' said the colossus, sounding muzzy. 'I'm fine. No worries. Fine. The bloody thing bit me!' As if this were entirely out of character for an enormous spider whose web they had plummeted into, like some sort of snack delivery service.

No wonder the trolls had given up the chase down this grim passage of death. Clambering up further, Clarence could see the big Northman stretched out, just off centre of the structure. Remembering their plummet now, he recalled bouncing. His diminutive form had meant that after the initial arresting impact with the main web, he had plunged on to smash into the scraps and refuse from previous meals that cluttered the base of this enormous shaft.

About fifty feet further up, he could see the smashed door dangling into the chamber, but the main shaft strung with webbing hither and yon disappeared up beyond the limits of his gaze.

Looking over at his friend, all was not well. Halvar rocked back and forth, eyes closed, his massive axe stuck fast several feet away from his groping right arm.

Clarence could now see that both hands held the fourteen-inch poniards he kept in his belt sheaths.

Looking down at the cooling corpse of the enormous beast, Clarence was astonished anew at the feral savagery of the barbarian. A knife fight against such a creature was impossible, surely a death sentence none could survive. And yet:

'I don't feel good… like a two-keg hangover.' said Halvar, with a wracking wheeze that Clarence did not like the sound of. The web fibres were less sticky at the edges of the construction. Time and dust meant the small thief could brace himself and balance against the wall, then look down on the prostrate figure. Halvar's usual weathered complexion, buoyant with life, looked sickly pale.

'Where did it bite you, Halv?'

'Hand.' came the reply. Halvar did not open his eyes to speak. The gnome saw with horror that the warrior's left wrist was at a strange angle; the scale mail gauntlet twisted, and half crushed where the beast had caught his hand in its mandibles. The wound looked bad, but not mortal. However, hanging in the air was the terror of poison.

'Stay here big man, I'll be back in a sec.' Clarence dropped down the wall he had just climbed as quickly as he could. Kicking back and forth amongst the cluttered floor, he examined the bodies looking for anything usable, Halvar needed healing now. The pack he had nearly tripped on yielded some ancient torches, so dry as to be almost desiccated. Clarence bound the tip with rag strips from the pack and a few moments of work with his tinder box, yielded a spitting yellow flame. He did not need it, but it would maintain Halvar's spirits and infravision was less effective in environments of uniform temperature.

The massive beast was curled on its back, barbed legs hooked in towards its abdomen and surrounded by the dregs of historic meals, it was a morbid sight. The predations of the enormous hunter had been varied, from web-wrapped, crusted rats and giant bat corpses to several hominids. He could not tell all species, but a couple of the bodies had been wearing metal armour, plate steel. So likely humans, others were perhaps kobolds from the looks of the skulls. Rummaging through the ancient canvas pack he found nothing of use. Some long-ago rotted iron rations, and a faded and cracked leather wineskin. No bandages, scrolls or potions.

Cursing he checked the twisted metal-clad corpses of the ancient fighters, but again nothing. One had a curiously carved ruby ring still on its mummified finger, which he pocketed for now. No bandages or potions. Still reeling from the impact of the fall, his mind finally kicked into action.

Healing potions! That was the answer, they had some! Veritas had them, in his pack, he had said so. The old man just had to get in here and...

The memory of recent events cascaded in his still muzzy brain, the horrific image of the priest's corpse, the hideous trolls rending him apart.

Clarence had liked the old buffer. The memory was painful but could not be altered now.

What about his pack?

Clarence thought he could recall it bouncing on the old man's back as he made his fateful charge. He looked up at Halvar and swallowed.

So, nothing to worry about then? Just sneak back into a troll pack's lair, on his own, and find the belongings of their most recent meal without them smelling him. Steal said belongings, hoping against hope that the contents were not smashed, finally high-tailing undetected back here before his friend died.

He almost laughed, what would Halvar say?

Easy!

Summoning his reserves of courage, Clarence wedged one of the torches into the wall at the bottom of the pit and clambered aloft to explain the plan to the trapped Northman. Halvar opened his eyes slowly when Clarence shook his leg then the big warrior listened in silence.

'How are you feeling now?' ended the thief.

'Like shit, got a headache…' said Halvar. 'I'm a bit tired, I think…' he started, then trailed off into a bubbling cough.

'Listen, my friend, you're Halvar. You're unstoppable, stay awake, ok? I'll be back as soon as I can with something to make you feel better.'

'Thanks, mate.' Halvar said phlegmatically. That was that. No panic, no terror, just a quick *'see you soon'* and Halvar was reposed.

Clarence climbed the cracked rock of the wall swiftly. Curling his fingers over the smashed door lintel, he heaved himself up and with a glance down at the faint red outline of the man below, took a moment to think. Trolls had an extraordinarily strong sense of smell.

How in Glasya's panties am I going to get in and out of that cave without them spotting me?

Assuming, of course, there was something still to find.

Deep gnomes had dark skin, and one of their natural defences in the deeps was to be somewhat camouflaged against earth and bare stone. Clarence looked down at his battered leather armour; it was not bad for sneaking, but it was suboptimal. He needed to be perfect. Quickly he stripped off his armour, sword belt and small pack.

Standing in his soft leather boots, even removing his undershirt and britches, he took stock. He 'washed' his face in the fine dust of the corridor floor, endeavouring to remove the spider blood. Most of which was on his armour in any case. His final consideration was whether to slip his sword's shagreen sheath over his shoulders so that at least he was armed. His mind conjured the image of the razor-clawed death machines... he decided against it.

If he got caught, he was dead.

Clarence could not hope to fight a group of trolls. Their wounds would certainly have healed by now.

Fuck it.

Better to roll the dice and hope someday to be able to tell the Guild Master about this. Clarence swore bitterly in several languages. Finally, with nothing but his loincloth and padded boots, he trotted through the lichen-lit doorway and into the chthonic black.

Chapter 6

'You are at a huge advantage, Boy, you're a midget!' called Bellof, smiling down at the angry gnome. Clarence did not snap back that he was the correct size or remind the Guild Master about his race. He respected Bellof and knew that he was being riled on purpose, to make mistakes and to simulate the stresses of a mission.

'I can see your fumbling from up here and I don't have infravision.'

That was harsh, and both knew it. The wiry middle-aged man with salt and pepper hair was standing on the sidewall of an alley staring down at him amidst the piles of stinking refuse. They were deep in the murky heart of The Mire. The area was a maze of narrow thoroughfares, alleyways, crime and society's rejects. No one wandered here by mistake, especially after dark. To be a denizen of the Mire was to rub shoulders with the seedy underbelly of the city. The assassin's guild was here, smugglers, kidnappers, whorehouses and of course thieves. Plenty had reason to visit, all had reason to be cautious. Anything could be arranged in The Mire if you knew who to ask and of course, had the gold to match your pernicious desires. People said the Duke should raze the place to the ground, but even the pampered aristocracy required a guild service on occasion. Many had needs, a burning lust for something, or someone.

Bellof had chosen this alley to use for his advanced shadow walking exam because, as Clarence now realised, the gibbous moon would rise and shine straight into it. As it had just done. The place was lit up like a harvest festival, it was almost impossible to find a patch of darkness, let alone hide in it.

'Back to the start, this time you fail.'

Trudging back to the junction with Wyre Street he glanced up to where Bellof had been, but the Master was no longer occupying his perch by the weathervane. Clarence had expected as much. Thin clouds scudded across the night sky, but they would not help. How to approach this then?

This end of the alley was crooked and so the right side was darker with shadow. The deepest gloom offered good patch-walking for the first thirty feet, but he was unsure how to proceed after the pile of overflowing bins.

He recalled what complaining about the fairness of a challenge had gotten him. Backstabbing lessons it had been. Thieves were not fighters, but on occasion, you needed to know where to shiv an obdurate guard. Clarence had studied the texts and knew where the arteries ran, knew the pressure points and the gaps in all armour types. His final test at the footpad graduation had been to silence a mark with a one-hit backstab.

The rumour was it was a human female. Could you bring yourself to do it? Was she secretly armoured, a dummy, an illusion or some other trick? All the scruffs had agreed that it was the big one!

Could you kill without knowing? Without compassion?

Clarence had not worried about a human woman, not his problem. This was where it was at, freedom! That came with consequences. He did not want to kill an innocent but had committed to his path. However they had gotten themselves in danger, was their lookout.

On the night, it had been perfect. Clarence had slithered up the wall and through the locked window, into the test zone of

51

The Continental. Avoiding all the usual gotchas; including the pressure trap under the lush carpet, he had moved like a ghost through to the final door. After oiling the hinges, he deftly picked it open. Slipping his sword from a velvet stealth sheath, he approached the large ballroom that was the designated killing space, ready to slay.

Clarence had double-checked for traps, only then entering the inner sanctum's beechwood door... where the mark was waiting.

It was a giant.

A fucking giant!

He was three feet and three inches tall, in his boots maybe an inch more. Twelve feet of hair-matted goliath was in front of him, its vast bulk obscuring the candlelight and throwing colossal shadows across the opulent ballroom. The creature was standing with its back to him, gawping at the glittering chandelier suspended from the arched wooden ceiling, playing with the chiming crystals like a moron.

In his exasperated fury, Clarence instinctively stepped sideways for a better view. Stepping, without first checking his footing. A floorboard creaked loudly. The hirsute brute had whirled, eyes hunting, its knotted club raised...

When Clarence awoke two days later, with his left side one enormous bruise and a broken arm, the assassin Ledgard calmly informed him that in fact, he was the moron. The lean, scarred man who had instructed them in stealth kills was standing over his cot with a pitiless sneer.

'If you're too low for the back, bring the back to you.'

'One strike!' Clarence had wheezed, the rules of the grading were explicit.

'Certainly,' the assassin replied, 'one finishing strike. However, you could have taken the tendons of both knees with the one slice before that, could you not?'

'Yes, but…' the battered gnome complained through bruise blackened lips before the grim man cut him off.

'Cheaters and tricksters win, Boy. It would appear rather that you… are a loser.'

The shame still burned him. Looking down the grimy alleyway, Clarence decided. It was a risk, and he was certainly cheating. He had avoided the rat traps and caltrops placed in the deepest puddles of black on his first attempt, but this time there would be none of that. Focusing his mind, he reached within to wrap himself in the darkness.

Psionics.

Clarence had learnt the name from the Guild library, although even that vast accumulation of leather-bound learning had little to tell. Since childhood, he had been able to affect little things. Sleight of hand, card tricks, but also things like other people's perceptions. It had made him mistrusted, suspected, and friendless.
Clarence had vowed to learn more about it, but never dared to tell anyone of his nascent skill for it would have scared

them, and the ultraconservative gnome society would consequently have shunned him.

The one tome he had discovered referring to it was a stolen volume from the Magic Users Guild. It claimed that there was a plethora of powers if you were strong enough to achieve mastery. Anyone could be a psionic according to the text; human, halfling or elf. Few had the gift. Fewer still knew how to focus it.

The Mages guarded their lore jealously, but some of the thief Guild Masters could penetrate the wizard's tower defences. It took time and money to decipher such snatched scripts, but the rewards could be great. Some even claimed they could replicate satisfactory magical effects from such arcane scribblings.

However, the relations between the Guilds remained cordial for annoying as this was to the spellcasters, they regularly needed spell components that were simpler purloined than honourably sourced. Clarence was hoping that mayhap he could utilise those relationships to broaden his investigation into the psionic arts as he climbed further in the Guild hierarchy.

More concerning was that the tome in question also carried portentous warnings. Perilous passages described the manifold evils that would hunt a psionic. That such a secret power made you a target. To some of these monsters, it made you a meal. Clarence had not liked the book's vividly painted illustration plates one bit; tentacle-faced fiends that lived in the deeps.

'Utter not their names, reader! Lest they steal more than your possessions…'

One day he would seek out more learning about it, but since then he practised nightly on his excursions into The Mire. The fewer people around, the easier it was. The more they were not expecting you, the simpler it became. He was not invisible; it *was not magic. Yet somehow, Clarence could affect the viewer's minds, causing them to ignore and disregard him.*

Focusing purely on the cloaking darkness and his mind's energy, Clarence padded from one end of the alleyway to the other passing directly through the moonlit courtyard. When he reached the farthest end of the route, he was sweating hard in the frigid air. The concentration levels still did not come easily, and he felt drained. Nothing moved and Clarence could hear just the background hum of the city. Knees sagging, he stepped into the shadows and dropped the cloaking.

'One day,' said a soft voice by his ear, 'you'll have to tell me how you did that.' Clarence started and whirled to face the thin figure in the darkness. The Master was looking down at him inscrutable, for a long moment he held the gaze. Then, leaning forward, Bellof pulled down the gnome's leather collar and pinned the coveted, ebon star to the inside, where it would not show.

'Welcome to your new grade, little burglar.'

Chapter 7

On velvet feet, the diminutive figure approached the last bend in the passageway before the troll cave. Crouched amongst the scraps of old meals, dirt and rubble Clarence stopped to listen. He could hear the grunts and barks that consisted of the trollish tongue; gnomes did not learn it what would be the point? He tried to estimate numbers, but other than more than two, he could not say.

Lying flat on the floor, Clarence inched forward until he could make out the heat signatures. The lichen glow was so faint that the bold pulsing reds and purples of the infravision stood out more than daylight vision. Three of the monsters stood about sixty feet away, another had its back to him doing something he could not make out. The rest were hunkered close to the broken doorway they had entered by.

It had occurred to Clarence that the backpack would be hard to see from any distance and that he would be best finding what was left of Veritas' body if he could track it down. That inevitably meant closing with the trolls. The big beasts were always hungry; it was a cliché, like a druid loving sheep.

Peering into the cold darkness near the shattered door frame, he noticed a part of the cave wall had collapsed. The debris pile was too small to obscure a man, but enough for him. On his belly, pressed hard against the rock wall, Clarence flexed his way over the hard earth floor, ribs searing with pain from his earlier fall. Ignoring the throbbing discomfort, he arm crawled swiftly, edging up to the cluster of ceiling fragments and stone shards that now blocked him from sight.

This was where Halvar slammed the second troll. The damp stickiness of spilt blood under his hands had a reek reminiscent of sewage, alien and foul.

Louder grunts from the heavy shadows ahead warned of a change. Clarence shrunk closer to the rockfall; the dusty gore-flecked rubble was enough so long as no troll walked directly past. In a sudden panic, he began to focus his powers of concealment, but the noise swiftly receded. He waited, immobile.

Silence.

If anything, the cave beyond felt empty now. Stealing a furtive glance, he saw exhaled heavily realising it was indeed so. The trolls had moved away beyond the craggy outcrop fifty feet down the passage.

He leapt to his feet, time to move. Weaving his psionics about him for whatever protection that would offer, Clarence slunk stealthily towards the troll's previous location, using all his prowess at silent movement. Skirting any loose gravel, rocks or other detritus, but there was nothing to be seen here. He was doing his best to keep one eye on the nexus of the next bend, whilst scanning for a battered leather backpack.

Ahead he could hear the trolls faintly, still moving away. If they came back, he knew he could never again pass them and view this newly revealed path. Their senses were too sharp. Clarence broke into a run. This was his one shot at eliminating that part of the search area.

At the next bend, the cave started to widen, the roof rising until it was at least fifty feet high. The lichen glow was diminishing, now but the floor and ceiling were covered with monstrous growths. Stalactites and stalagmites reigned in this cave; Clarence could hear the mournful drip of water in the blackness.

Straining his sight, he could just make out the thermal signatures of footprints. There were dim smudges of heat on the rock floor. The trolls had moved on. A smashed stalagmite to his right formed an opening in the otherwise near-impenetrable barrier of mighty extrusions that stretched from wall to wall and floor to ceiling. Clarence focused harder on the cave roof.

Was there also a smudge of illumination there perhaps? In that gap, just…?

Clarence sprinted to a huge shaft of limestone where a rock column had been accreted by the water of aeons. As quickly as he dared, he raced up it. It was slick, but no longer damp, and so he was able to ascend near to the jagged roof. It was a dangerous move, but better than heading blindly into the labyrinth of interlaced rock piles and ancient monoliths ahead.

Light!

He had been right. Perhaps five hundred feet ahead he could see the exit to the cave. It was tiny and not much sunshine made it through all this rock, but there was a hint of green out there. Scanning for the troll band, Clarence waited a minute or so as his sensitive eyes adjusted to the power of this distant daylight. Soon he could make out through the miniature portal they were high on a cliff; the verdant green was the dark emerald of evergreens. There was a valley below, he even caught a hint of sap from a zephyr of breeze lost in the rocks.

I can escape!

This was surely his best shot. He could easily hide in this maze of inky stone and get out when the trolls headed back to their lair. Or sooner if they had gone raiding. Whatever, this meant he did not have to face them in the narrow section near the splintered portal.

Clarence's sharp ears caught a growl that suggested the trolls were returning. Their guttural grunting was approaching fast, although sounds bounced strangely in these tangled warrens of stone.

His brain whirred:

Time to choose.

The spider had been massive, and no doubt the venom extremely toxic. Surely the barbarian was already dead. The swinging arms of the lead troll emerged from behind an escarpment of fallen rocks, fifty feet away. Its fur-matted scalp and lank, bat ears swivelled in the dim shafts of distant daylight.

The other fanged horrors followed close behind. No sign of even a limp on any of them, their clawed feet clicked the stone. Clarence could not even tell which had been injured.

No, they were too much for Halvar to take on even in full health. Much better to take this chance and get back to the city. He had money enough. Clarence shrank back into a crevice at the top of the pillar and wove his concealment around him.

This was *the perfect* opportunity.

He had not found the potions and anyway they were almost certainly smashed in Veritas' suicide charge. This was better. He had always been safer on his own. No companions or friends. Alone.

'Thanks, mate.'

He pictured Halvar rocking on the web, big trusting face pale in the torchlight...

'Oh *bollocks!*' he muttered.

Clarence leapt down the rock pillar at dangerous speed, cutting both hands and cracking his knee. He crunched hard into the gravel-strewn path before vaulting back to his feet, and without a backward glance at the approaching death, sprinted into the gloom.

Chapter 8

'Hey, wake up! Wake up!' yelled the dusty, near-naked gnome sitting astride the enormous, armoured chest, the steel scales winking in the torchlight.

'Halvar, wake the fuck up you ungrateful bastard!' he slapped and shook him, finally emptying his water skin over the bearded face in exasperation.

'Hmm… huh?' sputtered the massive form.

'Oh, thank the gods,' he stammered, 'after all that...'

Halvar looked awful. Slate-grey, with deep yellow bags under his eyes. Veins bulged on his hands, neck, and forehead. Clarence had been sure he was dead.

Well, no time to lose.

Clarence had found Veritas' pack relatively undamaged not five feet from where the poor man had been ripped apart. The trolls had not moved, they had simply eaten him immediately. Even the skull had been smashed to access the tender morsels within.

It was with a surge of relief that Clarence opened the bag to see a selection of cloth-bound bottles nestled amidst the earthenware oil flasks.

Fleeing back down the fungus-lit tunnel, heat vision again in the ascendant, it occurred to Clarence that he had no idea which potion was which. Only the cleric had known.

Clarence knew little about magic but had heard that potions took a minute or so to take effect. The only other thing he was certain of was that it was dangerous to mix them… he really hoped this did not get messy.

'Ok, big man,' he said, 'pick a potion.'

Unperturbed, Halvar slowly shoved his enormous hand into the crumpled satchel and pulled out a clear vial. Raising it to his lips, he drank like parched desert sand.

Sitting on the tattered shreds of Veritas' cloak laid across the sticky web, Clarence held his breath. For long moments nothing happened. He stared, studied the sweating brow, the pasty texture… no change.

Then, the web around the recumbent barbarian slowly inched up into the air. Clarence took a moment to process this craziness. The big man was attempting to float up towards the distant shaft ceiling.

'Dammit, *Levitation*.' he spat.

Quickly Clarence pressed another glass phial into the warrior's outstretched grip. Once again, Halvar swallowed the contents in a single pull. Clarence thought about the times he had seen the man sink foam-crested beers at a similar rate. He watched intently, the only sound the creaking of the monstrous spider webbing, straining to keep the great form from wafting away.

Something bizarre was happening now. Halvar's huge arms looked less sunburnt and in a shocking moment, his thick beard sloughed away! The blonde tresses slid down the polished armour and disappeared through the web into the darkness below. Clarence jumped to his feet, wobbling wildly. The man before him could now be no more than eighteen years old. The lines of the forehead and around the eyes had vanished!

Glasya's tits!

Halvar had aged in reverse, by as much as a decade.

Fuck! he thought, *there had better not be any more of those or I'll need swaddling for this oaf.*

One thing that had not happened was any improvement in Halvar's pallor. The snakelike veins on his neck throbbed angrily and his creaking breath was still slow.

In for a copper piece…

Halvar was already grasping for another glass bottle. This clear potion followed the others into the Northman's stomach. Again, the desperate waiting, the gnome sweating despite the chill. Suddenly, there was a loud rumbling from beneath the scale mail. Halvar's stomach rose alarmingly, for a moment he looked pregnant. He roared in pain, the sound reverberating up and down the webbed shaft. Sounds like a gurgling waterfall continued intermittently for long seconds before his distended gut returned to normal size. Clarence with a shaking hand passed another bottle to the grasping grey hand.

No choice.

Who knew what that potion did anyway?

'Yeah, I'm not sure either,' said Halvar, 'my stomach feels weird.'

Stunned, the gnome tried to get his reeling thoughts together.

What the hell was this? Some sort of ESP or Telepathy?

'Could be,' said the big man still stubbornly locked in the dead arachnid's trap. Clarence watched with awe as the iron-constitution barbarian swallowed yet another potion. This time the effect was almost immediate. He seemed to be drinking the colour back into his anaemic hide. The rosy skin tone of the cheeks, the deflating arteries, and his breathing quietened to the usual level. Clarence placed a hand on Halvar's crushed wrist, feeling bones move beneath his hand he swiftly yanked the gauntlet free. It looked normal again, the skin was warm and vital.

'Halvar?'

The only response was a snuffling sound, then after a long pause, a snore. Clarence stared:

'No way...'

As the gnome swiped a wrist over his damp brow, Halvar began a steady cadence of loud snores. Then his stomach rumbled again but did not engorge. The webs continued to strain upwards, their sticky tendrils preventing the two-hundred-and-eighty-pound man-mountain from floating away. Clarence flopped back on the cloak, a smile dragging itself across his dusty, battered face.

'You have got to be kidding!' he sniggered as the snoring continued. His chuckling laughter built until its quivering transferred through the bobbing fronds causing the floating sleeper to bounce, to his further exhausted merriment.

Chapter 9

Bajan walked behind his leather-clad guard Gilen up the sharp gravel path that led to the escarpment. Small pieces of stone became stuck in the smooth pads of his feet and he cursed. The day was ending, and Bajan did not like being above ground before darkness was complete. Sometimes though, these tools needed direction. He wore dark orange robes lined with wolf fur, which kept him warm as he hurried along. There were outsiders loose, it would seem, he would soon put a stop to that.

'Pick up the pace,' he barked at the stooped, sharp-eared kobold accompanying him. Gilen's ragged chainmail jingled a little louder in the evening stillness as he lolloped ahead to the base of the ascent.

An ancient avalanche had coated this bleak granite cliffside with boulders. This meant that even though it was a long way to their destination, it was simple climbing up to the cave. Both Houndstooth Clan members were capable mountaineers anyway, Shaman and soldier.

Bajan had known the humans would send warriors out to eradicate them. The Clan raiding had become too profitable of late, in all sorts of ways. The wagons were big business, and the fools would not want to let that development go unchecked. He leered inwardly as he thought of the sport, they had been making with the captured human pups. He could write a scroll on the torments he had invented for them... how they bawled and screamed.

Maybe I should, he mused.

It was an enjoyable pastime, and the other packs would want to know. Plus, he had plenty of skin for vellum now.

His twitching wet nose picked up the troll stink before they were halfway up the rock face. It trickled down between the rocks, foetid and faecal, like a racked man's diarrhoea. He spat at the shadowy form of Gilen before him.

'Move faster, idiot. I want to be gone from here as soon as possible.'

Bajan hated the mop-haired eating machines, but they were useful if properly handled. It had been so simple to leave the fake trail up to Widow's Peak. Humans could not track for giblets; they used their eyes, the idiots! Altogether the stratagem had worked brilliantly.

Three nights past Bajan had watched from his scrub-covered warren mouth as the convoy of clowns rolled into the valley below. Four sand-coloured, canvas-backed horse carts. Not as many as expected, so much the worse for them. The pack had wanted to set on them the first evening. The humans were camped at the base of the rockfall and the pack had been keen to roll boulders down from above.

'No,' he had warned 'have patience.'

His way was better, surer. If the tin cans wanted to fight, then let them fight *Her*. The spectral hag was no friend to anyone, she scared even the trolls. No chance Bajan would go anywhere near her portentous dwelling, but he would show *them* the way.

The plan worked superbly. False paths and a weak ambush had cunningly sent these arrogant monkeys blundering into her black abode. None ever returned. True, it had required he sacrificed a few underlings to lead them, but the den bitches were always breeding. Plenty more pups in a litter.

Then some hours ago, the trolls had sent word that there might be a survivor. Bajan had not understood the garbled message exactly, but they had found two and killed one seemed to be the news.

The Widow was getting sloppy.

Bajan had come himself on this chilly evening, for if they could escape *Her*, then he might need to use his divine conjurations. The gifts of the Horned One were deadly indeed.

The survivor had fled down into the spider paths, but Bajan wanted to be sure it was finished. The trolls and his magic were both lethal, certainly enough for anyone they might discover. There must be no survivors, or their larger plans might come to nought. Men would fear the mountain Kobolds properly again very soon.

As they should.

Cresting the cliff way that led onto the exposed cave plateau, his panting breath misted in the frosty air. The swirling mountain breeze smelt of pine and imminent snowfall he thought, chestnut eyes flicking up to survey the bulging sky. Turning, Bajan regarded the dim valley laid out hundreds of feet below, snout ruffling in the wind. Looking over the endless conifers to the twinkling fire of the human's camp, he knew there was a hunt-pack taking the horses and supplies at this very moment.

He wished he could be there for the torments he thought, claws flexing on both hands. However, this was important and must be dealt with. Any risk this close to the den was unacceptable. Bajan tracked a single white flake in the dim light for some moments before he turned back to the cave mouth.

'Fetch them,' he snapped to the loitering guard, 'I'll wait.'

Trolls tended to attack first before thinking, so if they got a little *chompy*, he would make sure someone else took the brunt of it. What else were minions for?

He heard the trolls grunting and grinding their blasphemous words long before the three emerged from the cave mouth onto the high lip overlooking the valley. Piebald, bulbous and mangy, they disgusted him. The black fangs protruding from their upper and lower lips caused their words to be clipped and indistinct. They particularly struggled with vowels… or *vwlz* as they would say. Bajan was careful, nonetheless, to keep his face blank of the disdain he felt as they approached.

Grzzt was in front. The largest of the ugly brutes, his splotchy gut bulged as if he had been gorging himself. He tramped over the frozen earth, as gossamer snowflakes began to swirl between them. The pungent stench was as bad as ever, Bajan steeled himself to remember to talk dimwit. As Grzzt growled down at him, deliberately standing over the rippling-robed shaman to intimidate him, Bajan coughed out a question in the uncouth tongue.

69

'Rggr' the troll snarled back.

Bajan fumed. These morons had not gone to look for the survivor as requested. He must lead them, or rather goad them ahead of him – force them to find and finish this fugitive. There could be nothing else that would suffice, he must *see* the body. Bajan rasped out another question.

'Ygnnt trqzzz.' came the reply.

One man, with an axe. Simple enough, these creatures were too stupid to glean useful details or nuance that might be of assistance to him. Bajan was pondering how to begin the search when there was an explosion of light from inside the cave. Bright flickering lit the stalagmites as if a mighty fire were burning beyond his view.

What in the ninety-nine? Bajan started, turning to Gilen who was nearer the cave he shouted:

'What's happening, dolt?'

The guardsman glanced uncertainly at Bajan before finally bounding into the cave mouth, past the first of the towering menhirs that peppered the ancient cavity and out of sight. He subsequently barked in alarm.

'What's happening?' Bajan yelled again, striding forward as there was more raucous noise from inside the tunnel, echoing bellows and the sound of heavy impacts. Gilen returned at a full sprint, ears flat with terror. Bajan whined in surprise, as the mailed guard bolted back towards him.

He was about to shout again, demanding details, when shockingly dark blood fountained from the kobold's mouth. Gilen's tread faltered and he slumped to one side, face twisted by the flat blade sprouting from it. Gore spurted steaming in the frosty air, the point of the knife standing clear of the smashed ruin of the Gilen's face. Teeth rattled to the rock floor as he crumpled, wide eyes fixed on the shaman. Bajan backed frantically.

Grzzt shouted and the two other trolls responded by knuckling over towards the brightening cave. Putrid skin strobed by the pulsing orange emanations.

Suddenly, with a ringing shout, a burning revenant appeared at the entrance before them. Seven feet of incandescent fire stood sizzling and spitting in the night. Raising a coruscating arm, it pointed a blazing finger at the monstrous collective and thundered:

'YOOOOUUU!'

The moment held as they stared at this demonic newcomer, and then the tableau shattered, and it rushed to close with them at impossible speed.

Bajan leapt for the rocks at the side of the path; he could not believe what he was seeing. The two trolls were the first to meet the charging tornado of flame. Black smoke poured off it, tendrils of dirty fire cavorting up into the darkness. The apparition swung a separate column of incandescence that swept sparks through the black and impacted the lead troll. With an appalling crunch, the beast was picked up and hurled aside; green blood sizzled through the air.

Gasping, Bajan saw that the fanged monstrosities' hideous head had been severed! The blow had sliced through the neck and top of one shoulder, sending the remains tumbling.

Scurrying behind the nearest boulder, Bajan tried to take stock. It must be an elemental being of flame that assaulted them, by The Watcher's horns he had never seen the like of it.

The second troll lunged at the feet of the burning destroyer, trying to grapple, but misjudged the newcomer's prodigious acceleration. The fire figure pounced aside panther-like before the terrible blade again slammed down. The blow crushed bone and severed skin with a hiss. The searing blade bit through flesh and into the stone below, spattering thick blood across the virgin white snow. The troll's head rebounded up before it rolled clear of the pulsing, spasming body.

Bajan gathered himself: whatever this horror show was, he surmised that it must be some trickery of the survivor. The trolls would be up again soon he knew, but if it was indeed a man under there, then experience told him what to do. This idiot would soon be calling him master. Standing in the shadow of the flame-kissed boulder, he began to weave his magic, calling on the might of the Lord of Deception to deliver him some evil.

Meanwhile, Grzzt leapt to attack. He was confused, but also an experienced combatant as all trolls were. Just keep fighting, trolls always win in the end. Even with the hated flame's touch, his brothers would soon be up again. Their bodies twitched and shook even now. Distracted, he noticed that their heads were moving, bobbing away into the night, floating about two feet off the ground. He howled his savage rage: none of this made sense! In his bewilderment he made a choice, flinging himself at the onrushing conflagration of smoke and blade. Grzzt sprang.

The crash as they met shook and echoed through the mountain peaks. Black talons raked across the figure of fire. Smoke caromed around the pair, sparks zinged, and metal rang. The figure staggered as Grzzt's blows rained down, the enormous monster clubbing and ripping. The heat-miraged apparition swayed and darted in before leaping away. Again and again, the spitting, flame-trailing axe swung, parried and struck, moving with the speed of a serpent's tongue. The burning man and the beast weaved back and forth, scrabbling for advantage.

Grzzt was soon bleeding heavily from deep cuts on his arms and legs. It was merely a short-term problem, but it slowed his onslaught. Every attack was burning him, and his maddening hatred of that despised pain caused a mist to form before his eyes. The dancing light of the hellish djinn before him turned every nearby snow mote into a winking nova of sparkling brilliance.

Smoke filled his nostrils, piceous eyes wild as the blood lust took him completely. Foam flying from his snarling lips he leapt high to crush the figure to the floor. Grzzt would take months to heal from this fight, but the taste of salty blood was all he craved. He must rend and he must kill!

Standing behind his snow-dusted boulder, hands weaving complex sigils in the night, Bajan smiled triumphantly. Whatever this was, it would soon be his to control. He stepped forward to release the bewitchment, magic energy thrumming from claws to stubby horns. At his moment of vengeance, *Charm* in mouth, he froze, a dark black blade punched from his chest in a single stroke. An arm's length of graven steel glinted at him, his eyes blinked slowly back, fascinated.

Time slowed for Bajan as shuddering cold flowed towards his heart. Pain slammed with it; the sword blade had entered his back below the ribs on the left side, searing its line of agony through his lungs to smash his collarbone on exit. Bajan sank to the white-flecked ground, vapour rising from the blood pumping over his unfeeling hands.

With darkening eyes, he saw the flaming silhouette stagger towards the cliff edge, Grzzt held high above it, the troll writhing in the burning grasp.

What impossible strength!

Was his final thought, as with a victorious roar the beast was hurled like a meteor into the vertiginous void.

Epilogue

'Earth-shattering.'

'I suppose it was pretty loud.'

'It was fucking earth-shattering, alright?!'

'Ok, if you say so.'

Halvar looked smugly satisfied. His stomach
problems were an unusual side effect of the potion cocktail
Clarence supposed. Anyway, the big man seemed able
now to let rip with a sound like a calving mammoth, much
to his amusement. Halvar listened enraptured as the latest
flatulent boom echoed to and fro in the surrounding peaks.

Clarence laughed. Behind them, the bonfire of the
corpses burned with oily black smoke, hissing and spitting
at the descending snowflakes.

'How long left?'

'Next five minutes or that's my gem.'

'You're still counting?'

'Of course.'

'Logic, Titch. Long arms you see, he'll be way less
than five minutes.' said a singed Halvar, clothing scorched
and blackened. Clarence had advised him that the oil

should be fully extinguished before he took the ring off, but well…

The claws of the huge troll had rent Halvar's scale mail in several places, and he had purple and yellow bruises forming on the side of his brow. Despite this, the blood-crusted warrior seemed in remarkably high spirits. The *Ring of Fire Resistance* they had found in the spider pit had been a huge boon. The tiny, engraved flames had given it away, a real blessing.

Tricks can be the difference, he thought. *Play your hand to the full, but always take time to stack the deck.*

They were sitting on the mossy cliff edge, backs warmed by the noxious flame of the troll pyre, legs hanging above the drop. The huge man and the miniature man were snow-flecked and exhausted. Clarence peered down towards the valley floor; eyes scrunched against the wind.

'Did we get every bit of them on the bonfire?' he asked.

'Yep,' said Halvar.

'Well except that one little bit, I suppose.'

'True,' said the fresh-faced barbarian with renewed interest. He too stared into the windswept ravine; the trees now garnished with the final flurries of winter.
'Oh, by the way…nice of you to stop and steal gems, whilst I was busy fighting! Tells me a lot!' He rumbled bitterly.

'I gave you half!' said the gnome plaintively, reflecting how hard it had been to get the precious stones out of that carving on the dais. Concern creasing his brow, Clarence stared up at the huge shadow outlined against the flames. This was all rather unusual for Halvar.

Surely, we've been through too much to…

Halvar turned to him slowly, shoulders shaking.

'Got you!' he roared, tears rolling down his grin-split face. Clarence shook his head in exasperation whilst Halvar's booming laughter rolled over him, echoing out through the powder-flecked rocks, then sucked away into the tumbling, pillow-white slivers of ice.

Post-mortem

Grzzt's mind was gone, nothing but the need for blood and revenge remained. Feral instinct bespoke where it lay for him, so he continued to scramble up the snow-covered cliff. Blistered and charred yet within him pulsed yet enough vital energy to reknit the damage from his tumbling fall through the granite outcrops.

Bone had coalesced, bruised and rent skin had poured itself back together, scabbing and coagulating with perverse speed. The climb up the cliff had been tormenting, but rage and hunger drove him. Grzzt could now smell the dreadful oil smoke, now the tang of blood and now...

Knntz!

He salivated, the manling was still there!

Drool oozed between his champing fangs as he greedily sucked in the scent. Struggling to corral his desperate need to charge, Grzzt stealthily pulled his blotched torso over the lip of the cave. Midnight eyes roamed the clearing, hunting...

Then the booted feet of a leaping shadow slammed into his chest, jolting free his clawed grip on the stone. Grzzt bawled in frustrated torment. A blood-curdling howl hurled into the flake-filled night as he again toppled backwards over the ledge and plummeted.

'Double or Quits, Titch. This time he'll be faster. I want my gem back!' said a deep voice above him before it dwindled in the rushing air.

Gibbering with rage, Grzzt somersaulted gracelessly towards the jagged slabs below.

THE END

More by J.D Gammie

Dalliance With Devils

Halvar & Clarence journey south across the Prime of Pan-Terra, satisfied with their cache from the crypt of the spectre. However, travel proves problematic as they have been declared criminals by the vengeful Duke Manfred. Now, wanted dead or alive, they find unfamiliar refuge in the company of foreign nobility. This seemingly serene asylum may yet prove perilous, as the genteel games of the aristocracy shroud a spectacular secret that could shatter the peaceful concord of centuries, and spiral the City States into war! Mystery and mayhem await, in this, the first novel in *The Chronicles of Halvar and Clarence*.

Desert of Dread

Coming soon!

After the tumultuous events on the Baron's island, Halvar & Clarence sail south to the desert of Tular seeking adventure amongst the dunes. They find a cosmopolitan country under threat, whose centuries old merchant tradition has been violently disrupted by a new arrival: a dragon. Crucial clues to political machinations may be contained in the tome provided by Isabel, High Priestess of Torm, but distractions abound. With daring to be done and gold to be won, will our heroes do the reading before calamity overwhelms the continent? The search for glory continues in this, the second novel of *The Chronicles of Halvar and Clarence*.

Printed in Great Britain
by Amazon

20702675R00051